Sammy's Science Arizona

Chester Thompson

authorHOUSE®

AuthorHouse™
1663 Liberty Drive
Bloomington, IN 47403
www.authorhouse.com
Phone: 1 (800) 839-8640

Published by AuthorHouse

ISBN: 978-1-5462-5367-9 (sc)
ISBN: 978-1-5462-5366-2 (e)

Contents

Dedication

This book is dedicated to all of the students

of nature but especially to their brave mothers

who put up with their creature collecting.

THE EIGHT LEGGED PEST

E WALD CAME RUNNING IN YELLING, "Dad Randy was stung by a large scorpion"!
"Where is the scorpion right now", asked Sammy?
"Oh, I killed it with a piece of wood", said Ewald.

Sammy went out to where Randy Raccoon was sitting and looked at the dead scorpion closely. He discovered it was a Giant Hairy scorpion which is rare in the area because they prefer the saguaro forest where they eat centipedes, spiders, and other scorpions.

"Well I will take you to the hospital but this giant is only mildly poisonous so you will be alright", said Sammy.

"How can a scorpion that big be only mildly poisonous", asked Ewald?

Sammy decided to teach the boys about the four most common Arizona scorpions while driving to the hospital.

"It's not because of it's size Ewald. It is however the least poisonous of the four most common scorpions in Arizona", said daddy skunk.

"How many types of scorpions are there anyway", asked Randy?

"Actually our state is know for a variety of scorpions. They thrive in our type of climate but tend to be located mostly in the southern parts of Arizona", said Sammy.

"I heard you say that when you lived in Phoenix you would check the insides of you shoes before placing them on your feet", remarked Ewald.

"Yes I did. We also checked our beds for scorpions when we lived in an area where they were often found in houses", said Sammy.

"If the one that stung me was only mildly poisonous, what are the other three most common ones", asked Randy.

"The venom is meant to kill their prey which is mostly their size or smaller. Which means that deaths from a scorpion sting happens rarely. Now the Arizona bark scorpion is yellowish in color but in high elevations it is often stripped. Also it has long slender tail with the stinger at the tip", said Sammy.

"This is the one that is typically found in their houses by home owners in Arizona. These are also some of the most venomous of the scorpions in our state. They get their name from the fact that you can find them in and around tree bark and rocky desert areas", continued daddy skunk. This is the guy I looked for in my shoes and bed.

"I think I will also look in my shoes", said Randy.

The most common scorpion found in Arizona is the stripe tail. They are yellow in color with dark stripes on the top side. They do on occasion find themselves in homes but they normally live under rocks. The males are normally under 3 inches with the females being the bigger of the two. "I turned over a rock when I visited my grandfather in Phoenix and "I found one that my teacher said was a stripe tail scorpion", said Randy.

"They are very common in that area as well as other counties in Arizona", said Sammy.

The yellow ground scorpion is very much like the bark scorpion in appearance and is often mistaken for it. The biggest difference in their appearance is the yellow ground scorpion's first two tail segments are as wide as they are long. These scorpions are found in southeastern Arizona.

The giant hairy scorpion is the largest scorpion in the United States. That is the one you have already met. It gets its name from the dense hair coverage. While their appendages are yellowish their body color is normally dark.

"Here we are guys. Lets get you in to see a doctor", said Sammy. Later back at the tree house Randy was doing very well and had no ill effects at all. Tremor mouse didn't like scorpions even more than he didn't like cats.

All was quiet in the old oak tree house.

THE COWBOY TREES

ONE FINE DAY IN MAY Sammy called the boys in and asked them if they were up to another camping trip. Ewald being a road runner was always up for a trip anywhere. His only problem on a fishing trip was he never had the patience for fishing but then this wasn't a fishing trip. Erasmus being a porcupine had a lot of patience and was ready for a bit of adventure.

"Why don't you guys go see if Eddie beaver and Randy raccoon would like to go along for our camping trip", said Sammy daddy skunk.

"Maybe Momma would like to go this time, why don't you ask her", asked Ewald.

"No, she doesn't like camping unless we can take the whole house along", laughed Sammy.

"Dad is right Ewald, momma won't go camping", injected Erasmus.

The guys took off to ask their friends if they would like to go on the camping trip to the desert near New River. Randy told Ewald that he would ask his mom. Randy's mother said it was okay. Eddie told Erasmus that he couldn't go because he had too much work to do. When they returned home they told Sammy that Randy was the only one of their friends that could go on the trip. So Sammy took the rest of the day getting things ready for their excursion into the desert. Daphne momma skunk filled a back pack with canned beans, canned chili, potatoes, plenty of buffalo jerky, powdered eggs, bacon and corn on the cob. Then in another back pack she put tin cups, coffee, tin plates, plastic silverware, pots, an iron frying pan and some wooden matches. This was loaded into the truck. Sammy also put several cases of bottled water, their sleeping bags, the big tent and sturdy walking sticks into the truck. They were now ready to leave early the next day.

They awoke at 4 o'clock in the morning all ready to head out after a good breakfast of homemade biscuits and peppered gravy with bits of sausage chopped up in it. Then after saying goodbye to Daphne momma skunk they were off on their adventure. Traffic was light all the way to New River so the four of them made great time. Once they left interstate 17 Sammy drove to the location where they would set up their camp. After the tent was up and the rest of the camp was in order Sammy decided to take the guys on a hike around the area. It was Ewald that noticed a big lizard climbing up a mesquite tree near the trail and told everyone else to look.

"What kind of lizard is it and is it dangerous", asked Ewald.

"That is called a chuckwalla and no it's not dangerous", said Sammy.

"Can you tell us more about them", asked Randy.

So Sammy had the boys stop for a rest so he could give them more information on the chuckwalla. He began with, they are a species of large lizard that has a stocky build. They have a thick scaly tail.

"I have seen a few before but they were more orange in color", said Randy.

Sammy continued, their skin color does vary depending on the region they live in. Some are brown, others are gray, that one was blackish, but they have all have colored areas of red, yellow, pink, or orange.

"I read that the are herbivores and eat various types of plants," said Erasmus.

"They eat flowers and fruits when they are in season in their local area. Also the tender parts of desert plants. In fact they especially like the fruits of the prickly pear cactus," said Sammy.

Then going on with the facts, they eat early in the morning and bask in the sun most of the day usually on rocks. But if disturbed they dart into a rocky crevice, where they inflate their bodies and are difficult to get out. Some of our Arizona native Americans use to eat them.

"That sounds gross," said Ewald and Randy.

"Not if you can't find anything else to keep you from starving," said Erasmus.

Sammy suggested that they get moving. So the four guys continued on their way past the rocks and mesquite trees. Then they walked into an area where several saguaro cacti were rowing. They found a skeleton of a dead saguaro and picked up the wooden remains and carried it back to the camp.

"So this is what a saguaro cactus skeleton looks like," said Ewald thinking it would be great to take to his science class when school starts.

"What is so special about an overgrown, spiky plant anyway," asked Randy.

Sammy pulled out four folding camp chairs from the back of his truck and placed them near the fire pit they dug.

"Sit yourselves down on these chairs and I will tell you all about what makes them so unique," said Sammy while he started a fire for cooking their lunch.

"Personally I'm more interested in what we are having for lunch," announced Erasmus the porcupine.

Sammy laughed and said, "Well I guess we vote on lunch or facts about the saguaro. All in favor of facts raise your hands".

Even tiny Tremor mouse raised his hand even though he knew that it would not be seen. Tremor was always up for a story factual or not. Just before they pulled out of the driveway, he managed to get into the back of the truck so he could be a part of this adventure. After all he really liked Sammy's stories and his lunch didn't need cooking. Erasmus was the only vote for lunch. But Sammy decided to prepare the food while he told the facts about the tall cactus. Tremor sat himself on a flat rock behind the truck tire nearest to where Sammy sat so he could hear every word. The cowboy tree as momma skunk's brother called them when he was very little and saw one for the first time, is not actually a tree at all as you guys already know.

The cactus in its early stage is very difficult to locate because it is often under a Palo Verde or Mesquite tree. These are called 'nurse trees' by human botanist and cactus growers. Saguaros are extremely slow growers. In fact during their first eight years of life hey only grow to about one and a half inches tall.

"Now that is slow going for sure," said Erasmus.

"Yeah it sure is slow," said Randy raccoon.

"If you think that is slow listen to these facts. Its longest growth period is the transition from an un-branched cactus to a branched one. It takes about 50 - 100 hundred years before it grows its first branch and they are thirty five or so before they can flower," said daddy skunk.

"Whoa, 100 years to get their first branch. That is old," exclaimed Randy.

"How long do they live? Do they reach one thousand years old," asked Ewald.

"No, they die at about one hundred and seventy five though some have been known to live to be two hundred years old," answered Sammy before continuing his lesson on Saguaros.

They only grow in the Sonoran Desert of Arizona and Mexico. Arizona made the flower of the saguaro its state flower.

"They look very heavy, so how much does a full grown one weigh and how tall do they get," asked Erasmus.

"Adults can weigh up to six tons and grow to about sixty feet tall. However when rain is plentiful and the cactus is fully Hydrated even a younger one can weigh in at up to nearly five thousand pounds. Remember they are made up mostly of water," answered Sammy before continuing his facts. Humans who don't know any better plant them near their garages, houses, and driveways because they look western. This causes the saguaro to become possibly dangerous.

"Why is that," asked Ewald.

"I have seen a house smashed in half, a car crushed and a garage nearly destroyed because a two thousand pound saguaro died and fell on them. Most natives or people who have been in Arizona for several years know that there are cacti that can be as dangerous as many animals. The saguaro is very important to the Sonoran ecosystem because a lot of creatures use it as a host plant. For instance the Arizona state bird which is called the cactus wren often use the holes exposed by the Gila woodpecker in the saguaro skin making it a prime nesting area. The state of Arizona has passed laws protecting the cactus making it illegal to remove a saguaro from private or public land without a permit.

"So your saying that if I owned this piece of land I couldn't remove the saguaros to build a house on it," asked Randy.

"Not without a permit you can't," answered Sammy.

"Is there a bigger cactus in the United States," asked Ewald.

"The answer to that question is no," said Sammy.

"I wonder if mice use the saguaro as a home," thought tremor.

Sammy began to cook their lunch which was some very good chili and tortillas with cheese. Tremor kept an eye out for a dropped piece of cheese to go with his piece of jerky he found in the truck. After cleaning up from lunch the guys set out to hike in the other direction from their camp. On the way between some big rocks

Sammy suddenly stopped and said, "Turn around slowly and go around these rocks".

"Why," asked Ewald?

"Rattle snake," answered Sammy.

"I thought I heard a familiar sound," said Erasmus.

The fellows turned and made their way around the rocky area. They hiked quite a long way when Randy said, "I think I found a piece of old pottery". Sammy took it, looked it over and said, "Yes it is old and it is part of a Hohokam pot".

"What is a Hohokam," asked Randy.

"Well the Hohokam people were Arizona's original population of native Americans. There is evidence that these people used the ribs of the saguaro cactus to help in building the walls of their homes," said daddy skunk.

That night after dinner and after they were partially packed to head home, the guys sat around the campfire cooking marshmallows. The next morning Sammy got up made a quick breakfast for everyone before getting the boys up. After breakfast the guys finished packing up the truck for the return trip home. Tremor was already in the back of the truck. This he thought would help keep anyone from seeing him or accidentally leaving him behind.

"I have no desire to be left here with a rattle snake nearby," thought Tremor.

When they did get home they had a lot to tell momma skunk and Eddie beaver. Tremor would also have a lot to tell Donkey Dan about the adventure in the desert. Everyone was tired and fell asleep quickly in spite of the coyotes calling to each other. And all was quiet in the old oak tree house but not out in the desert.

ARIZONA'S TARANTULA AND IT'S FLYING ENEMY

O NE MORNING IN LATE JUNE while Sammy was reading in the living room and Daphne was doing some house work there was a knock at the front door. Erasmus yelled that he would answer it because he was expecting Eddie beaver over for a game of chess. Ewald and his pal Randy were outside in the pasture with donkey Dan. The two boys were tossing a baseball back and forth. Old Bonkers the orange tabby cat was taking a cat nap lying in the sun coming through the living room window. Tremor was outside next to the back porch collecting seeds to put in his food storage room. He liked being ready for the coming winter ahead of time. He spent the months of July to October collecting tidbits to store so he would have food for the entire winter. Actually he could never run out of food because he found food dropped on the floor under the table after every meal. Suddenly Sammy's reading was interrupted by Ewald and Randy running through the kitchen across momma skunks wet floor. The boy's were in a hurry to get to the living room and Sammy. Momma skunk was yelling for them not to run inside the house and stay off the wet floor. But they were in such a rush that like most ten year olds they didn't pay attention to her.

Once in the living room Randy excitedly said, "Sammy we found a very large spider in the pasture". "Dad it could be dangerous so can you come with us and take a look at it," asked Ewald?

Daddy skunk realizing that he wouldn't be allowed to continue reading his book until he went with them simply said, "Okay". So he got up placed his book down on the end table and started for the back door. That's when Daphne skunk came in and asked, "What is all the fuss about, is something wrong"?
"The boys found a large spider out in the pasture and they want me to take a look at it," answered Sammy.
"Well make sure it stays out there, you know I don't like spiders," said momma skunk. Ewald and Randy took Sammy out to the area of the pasture where they last saw it. But it wasn't at the same spot but they found it just a little further away. Sammy knew what it was as soon as he saw it.
"Let's leave him alone and go back into the house," said daddy skunk. On the way to the house Randy asked, "Exactly how dangerous is that spider anyway". Before reacing the door Sammy said, "In spite of it's bad rap, the Arizona desert tarantula is actually docile, though it can bite if it so desired". Continued Sammy, "Some people keep them as pets while others are very fearful at the Sight of one".

When they entered the house Sammy went directly to his favorite chair and said, "A person would really have to harass the Arizona tarantula to provoke it to bite them. And even then its venom is way too week to harm a person."
"That's great news, "said Randy.
"But they sure are ugly creatures," said Eddie as he sat down next to Erasmus on the couch.
"Their momma doesn't think so," added Erasmus smiling.

When everyone was finished laughing, Sammy continued. So you see apart from their looks there isn't anything to fear from it. Daphne walked in and said, "The tarantula might be harmless to us but I still don't like them and I especially will not have one in my house". Sammy knew right away that what she just said was so Ewald wouldn't get any ideas about having it for a pet. Tremor who was behind the grandfather clock was listening intently and said, "I don't want one inside either."

"I guess momma is afraid of spiders," said Ewald.

Sammy only smiled and began telling more facts about the tarantulas.

World wide there are perhaps hundreds of species of tarantulas. Some like our Arizona tarantula are not deadly while other species are deadly. You might hear people call the Arizona species the 'Desert Tarantula' or the ' Arizona Blonde Tarantula' the Arizona species is not deadly, "Just ugly," said Daphne. Sammy couldn't resist and said, "They say that beauty is in the eye of the beholder".

Then he continued with the facts. If you were an insect, a scorpion, or a small rodent like a mouse its venom could overcome you and you would be paralyzed.
"Now I know that I don't want one in the house," said a shivering tiny mouse behind the clock.

Bonkers who was still cat napping in the window heard the faint squeaking of Tremors comment and walked over to the grandfather clock sniffing around it. The one in our pasture is a male and you can tell because males are thin and lankier with black hair covering most of their body and reddish hair on their abdomen. The females have a more stocky body and they are covered in a light brown or tan hair. I'm sure you noticed that like most spiders they have eight legs and two shorter leg look a likes that are called pedipalps which they use for touching and moving their prey. The hair on it's abdomen are urticating hairs, which means they are barb covered hairs that come off to form a protective cloud. When contact is made these hairs can penetrate and irritate the nose and eyes of any would be attacker.
"So they are kind of like a porcupine in two ways, their hair is a weapon and they are ugly" said Ewald teasing his brother.
"Ewald stop picking on your brother," scolded Daphne.
"Yes Mom," answered Ewald.
"Actually some predators will go out of their way to avoid the spider,".
"Wow that is some weapon," remarked Randy.
"Having that happen wouldn't be very much fun at all," said Eddie.

Sammy who was wanting to get back to his reading didn't comment but just continued on with his science lecture. All of our north American tarantulas live in the southern and southwestern states.
"The one we found had dark hair so he had to be a male right," asked Ewald.
"That is correct Ewald," said Sammy.
"Dad already told us that earlier Ewald," said Erasmus getting even for the earlier ugly comment about him.
"Just making sure I understood him correctly," said Ewald.
"You boys need to stop interrupting your father and let him finish so he can get back to his book," said momma.

The males only live for ten to twelve years while the females can live up to twenty five years of age. As soon as the male reaches adulthood at about ten years old they begin searching for a mate. If he doesn't get squashed crossing a road or die because he is openly exposed so his enemies can see him, he dies soon after he mates.

He also must be careful that his mate doesn't make a meal of him and that occurs often. He can reach the body size of four inches not including the legs. Some of his enemies are large predatory lizards, snakes, spider eating birds, foxes and of course coyotes. They are nocturnal hunters of almost all insects and although it is very dangerous for them, they do kill scorpions. Their worst enemy however is the dreaded tarantula hawk, a large black wasp with orange wings. that specifically hunts tarantulas. This killer attempts to sting the spider. If successful, the sting paralyzes the tarantula. Then she lays her eggs on the spider and seals it up in a burrow. Then the poor tarantula becomes a meal for the wasp grubs to eat after they hatch out of their eggs.

"I hope our guy doesn't wind up baby tarantula hawk food," said Ewald.

"I hope I don't wind up spider food when I'm out in the pasture some night," said the still shaking mouse from under his bed.

Everyone left the living room so Sammy picked up his book and began where he left off.

And all was quiet in the old oak tree house.

A VISITOR AT ONE O'CLOCK

I T WAS A NICE SEPTEMBER day in Arizona's high country at the red rock area of Sedona. Sammy took the boys and their friends on a camping trip to that area. The evening was cool but nice as long as they had a campfire burning. It gets cold at night even in the southern desert areas of Arizona if you're not near a city or town. Sammy often said the houses, black top paved roads and parking lots make the cities stay hot at night. But he always noticed that the farther away from those things the cooler it gets at night.

They put two tents up and had dinner before settling into their tents for the night. Ewald, Randy, and Sammy were in their sleeping bags in the big tent. In the meantime Erasmus and Eddie Beaver were in the smaller tent fast asleep in their sleeping bags. About one o'clock in the morning Randy had to get up and look for a tree to water to relieve himself. He came back whispering I think that there is a bear in our camp but when nobody reacted he shook Sammy awake.

"I think I saw and heard a bear in our camp just as I got back to the tent," said a slightly nervous raccoon.

"Okay I'll go outside and check it out," replied a half asleep Sammy.

As he walked around the camp and circled the tents, he could smell an odor that he had smelled once long ago in the forest. However he couldn't recall what had created that odor so many years before.

"I'm not sure what it was but it's not out there now so how about we go back to sleep," said Sammy yawning.

The rest of the night went peacefully and they began getting out of their sleeping bags at six o'clock. The first one up was Sammy and he started a fire and made some coffee. Then he started to cook some bacon and scrambled some eggs. Erasmus and Eddie came out of their tent and saw Ewald and Randy looking at something on the ground by the tent.

"What are you two looking at," asked Erasmus.

"Last night when I got up to urinate I heard something in our camp. I thought that it might be a bear," explained Randy.

"Did you wake up my dad and tell him about it," asked Erasmus.

"Yes but when he went out to look whatever it was had gone away and everything was quiet," answered Randy.

"Anyway like I have already asked you, what are you guys looking at, repeated Erasmus.

"We are looking at an unusual foot print in the soft dirt by your tent,' said Ewald.

"It must have been quiet walking by our tent because I never heard a noise," said Eddie.

Sammy called them to breakfast and they filled up because camping and hiking makes a person hungry. When they finished Sammy said, "Let's have a look at the tracks you found". "Ewald said, "Dad, they're not bear, mountain lion, deer or even wolf tracks and in fact I don't think I have never seen tracks like these before". Sammy looked at the three toed tracks and said, "I have seen these tracks before".

"What made them dad," asked Erasmus.

"Why don't we go sit on the old logs by our camp fire and I'll give you all the information I know about the creature that made them," said Sammy.

So everyone walked over to the tree logs by their camp fire and sat down to listen. Even tiny Tremor the mouse who had hidden himself in one of the backpacks before they had left the house and was now inside the hollow log Sammy was on. The wee mouse always loved Sammy's stories especially the science ones. Sammy began; Some people call these creatures "cute", but actually the track you found is from a Javelina which is a rather ugly animal that produces a very unpleasant musky odor. This is why some people call them "Musk hogs or musk pigs". They are called other names as well even Arizona wild pigs but the word Javelina is the most common one. In fact they aren't wild pigs at all and in fact they are actually members of the 'peccary' family.

"When I was younger I heard that they were related to the rodents but since then I studied them more and now I know that they aren't related to rats, rabbits and the like. But sometimes I tell people that they are just to see if they know better or will study to find out for themselves," said Sammy smiling.

Most un- knowing humans think that it is a very hairy wild pig with razor sharp tusk. Pigs are from the old world and peccaries are from the new world. They inhabit central and southern Arizona, south east Texas, New Mexico, all the way southward through Mexico, central America, south Argentina. They love desert and semi desert areas best of all where there is plenty of cactus and other desert vegetation to munch on. They can be found resting in the shade of mesquite trees, Palo Verde trees, and rocky outcroppings especially along washes during the heat of the desert day.Their musky odor comes from a scent gland located on top of their rump which is covered by long hairs. This odor is the reason why some people call them 'musk pigs'.

They rub their scent on rocks and trees to mark their territory to warn away other herds of peccaries. These collard peccaries are very hairy and are one of three species of new world peccaries. Their color is peppered black, gray and brown with a faint white collar around their shoulders hence the name collard peccary.

"How big do they get," asked Eddie.

"When full grown they weigh in at 35- 50 pounds," said Sammy.

Then continuing the males are slightly larger then the females. Javelina are able to breed at about ten months old and they do so at anytime of the year and have two litters a year. "How big are the babies when they are born," asked Randy.

"Newborns weigh around one pound and start out a reddish color but attain the color of an adult at three months," said daddy.

Their herds can have up to fifty members but the norm is about ten - twenty. Their life expectancy is around twenty five years. The Javelina is most active at night when it is cooler. He eats cactus, mesquite beans, grasses, berries, roots, and dog food if you leave it outside. Garbage containers and flower beds are also fair game. Even though they are classified as herbivores they have small rodents, birds, insects and lizards on their menu also.

"What another mouse eater," squeaked Tremor.

"Are they dangerous," asked Ewald.

"Human tourist that visit Arizona think that these, Pig - like creatures the size of a medium sized dog are harmless. In fact they often feed them," said Sammy.

Then he continued to answer the same question by saying, "These gentle looking and slow moving Javalina are deceiving. They can become very vicious and aggressive on a moments notice seemingly for no apparent reason. They have been known to kill dogs and do a lot of harm to humans as well," said Sammy.

"I heard that they can pass along diseases such as rabies," said Erasmus.

"Yes they can," said Sammy.

They have very bad eye sight but a great sense of smell which can be used to find what the may perceive to be a threat. If they charge they can do some serious damage with the sharp and long incisors.

"As you already discovered from the tracks they have three toes on their hooves. They have bulky bodies and short legs attached to those three toed hooves," said Sammy.

"You said that they are hairy, is it soft hair," asked Ewald.

"No it is very bristly hair," replied daddy skunk.

"Perhaps we had best not go out after dark like I did, at least while we are here," stated Randy.

"That is a good idea," said Sammy.

"I'm not going out until the sun is up. I have no desire to be a meal for one of them," said Tremor

And all was quiet in the camp later that night.

THE MONSTER OF ARIZONA

S AMMY WAS SITTING IN HIS chair reading the morning newspaper and Bonkers the cat was laying by the warm fire burning in the fireplace. It was begging to get cold because it was nearing the Thanks Giving Holiday. Ewald and Erasmus along with their friend Eddy Beaver were outside feeding the chickens, goats and donkey Dan. They were also checking the water trough. When the boys entered so did the wee mouse Tremor because he knew someone would get Sammy started on a story of some sort. Daphne was in the kitchen preparing their breakfast. Tremor went behind the grandfather clock and sat on his thimble to eat some nuts, seeds and a piece of cheese he found under the table after their dinner last night.

"Dad what is a Gila Monster", asked Ewald as he sat on the couch.

"The Gila Monster is the largest lizard in North America and the only venomous one also", instructed Sammy.

"Exactly how large is it", asked Ewald picturing a car sized poisonous reptile in his young roadrunner mind. The normal adult size is about 16 to 24 inches and they can weigh around 5 pounds.

"That isn't very large", said Eddy.

"Perhaps not but it is very deadly", answered Sammy.

Then Sammy began his Gila Monster facts. The colorful lizard is unique to the southwestern states like Arizona, and New Mexico but it has a relative that lives in parts of northern Mexico. This Mexican counter part is called the Mexican Beaded Lizard. The Gila is colored with brilliant vivid orange, yellow and pink markings on a black body. It is a very threatened animal that is diminishing in numbers but it is federally protected and illegal to capture or kill one. Its head is large and he has small beady eyes. His tail is fat, short and used for fat storage so that they can go months between meals. They mostly live on a diet of eggs, other reptiles and birds especially the newly hatched.

"Can it kill a person with its venom", asked Erasmus.

"The bite is very painful and serious but is often not fatal. The last known death was reported in 1939. But then I have hiked through the desert most of my life, from fourteen years old but I'm 74 now and have never seen one in the wild while hiking. This could be because of the decline in their population as well as the possibility that they bite very few people. He is a very secretive reptile living about 95% of his life underground in burrows also he is slow and not real aggressive. They say that in order to be bitten you would almost have to pick one up. Once in your hands or near it a Gila Monster can very quickly bite you. And it hangs on strongly so don't touch it if you see one."

"I certainly would stay far away from one if I ever saw one", remarked a squeaking Tremor mouse.

"Are their young born or do the hatch out of eggs", asked Eddie.

"They are egg layers that normally lay 5 eggs to a clutch but can lay up to 12 at a time. They lay their eggs during June and August of the next year after they breed which is in may and June. Their eggs hatch out in April to June", answered Sammy.

"Isn't that unusual", asked Erasmus.

"Actually it is because no other North American lizard that lays eggs over-winters them and hatches them out the following year", said Sammy.

Daphne called and said the breakfast was ready. Sammy invited Eddy to stay for breakfast.

And all was quiet in the old oak tree house except for the sound of the forks.

DON'T HUG THE TEDDY BEAR

ERASMUS WALKED INTO THE LIVING room and lopped down on the couch and asked, "Dad do jumping cacti really jump? Some of my friends at school say that they do, but how can a plant really jump at you?"

"Let me tell you the real facts about the jumping cacti", said Sammy.

Just then Ewald came in and sat down next to Erasmus. Tremor the wee mouse ran behind the old grandfather clock and sat on his thimble to wait for the coming story. Sammy began by saying, "Actually there are two cacti called jumpers: 1) Is the Opuntia Fulgida and number 2) is the Opuntia Bigelovll also called the Teddy Bear Cactus". "Which one is it that grows in Arizona", asked Ewald

"Both of them do", replied Sammy.

Then he continued his lecture by saying, it is actually a myth that they actually jump. The teddy bear grows from 100 to the 3000 foot level on mountain slopes or hills. The other one grows from the 1000 to the 3000 foot level. Both are bad news for anything passing to close by them. The name teddy bear came from the fact that this cactus looks like its fuzzy, soft and cuddly like a teddy bear. In our Arizona sun they shine golden however once you have been stuck, you learn to keep at least a foot or more from the plants and watch for the joints that lay all over the ground nearby the plants. Even though they do not jump their bite is extremely painful.

"I think I would rather be chased by old Bonkers the cat than be anywhere near a jumping cactus", squeaked Tremor a bit loudly. Bonkers heard him and walked over to the grandfather clock and meowed "I would rather chase you then get near a jumping cactus".

Tremor ducked under his bed where he felt safer even though the cat couldn't get into his mouse house behind the clock anyway. Bonkers knowing this still liked putting a scare into the little mouse. Finally he decided he did enough and went back to his window.

"When will I ever remember to speak softly so Bonkers can't hear me," said Tremor.

Meanwhile Sammy was still speaking. The spines are vicious, strong, and barbed making them very tuff to remove from the hapless victim of the attack by the teddy bear.

The reason they came by the name jumping cactus is because their joint attachment is very loosely connected to the plant. The joints will attach to any helpless passerby as they even so slightly brush over the teddy bear cholla.

"Good thing we don't have one in our yard", said Ewald.

"Yeah or anywhere nearby here", added Erasmus.

Continuing Sammy said, "I fully agree boys".

By the way it does not matter even how slight of a brush which is why people believe the cactus jumps at them. They just simply do not feel the slight brush but they scream out in pain and think it jumped on them.The cholla does bear fruit but unlike the fruit of the prickly pear cactus, these fruits are not edible.

"So why does anyone get close enough to get stuck", asked Ewald

"They are what the old cowboys used to call green horns, that is people that are new from outside of our state, or too young to know better", said Sammy smiling.

"Well I guess they learned the hard way if they were stuck by a jumper", remarked Erasmus.

"That is why when your new to an area you need to ask what is dangerous in that area", said Sammy.
"But who should you ask about plants like cacti", asked Ewald.
"You could ask a university or the forest service", answered Sammy before he continued his narrative.

Those loose joints are not just for defense against anything that gets too close to the cholla but will brake off and fall to the ground where some take root and grow new cacti. You see their fruit is sterile so it just rots instead of reproducing by seed. The flowers are beautiful and the cacti blooms in February to may with greenish- yellow flowers at the end of the stems.

The boys got up from the couch and went out to find their friends Eddie and Randy. Momma skunk came into the house carrying two bags of groceries and went back out to bring in more. Tremor came out from under his bed and snuck out to the orchard to search for food. Sammy joined Bonkers in a cat nap.

And all was quiet in the old oak tree house.

WHAT'S SHAKING

SAMMY WAS AT THE DINNING room table writing his nature segment for the Sunday Donkey Dan radio broadcast. Sammy and Daphne took turns doing the live show. Erasmus was out in the pasture collecting insects for a school science project. Ewald was over at Randy's house most likely ridding their bikes. Bonkers was lying in front of the old grandfather clock because he heard a noise coming from behind it. Daphne was washing the lunch dishes. The old oak tree house was peaceful until Erasmus entered all out of breath from running.

"Dad I saw a snake in our pasture a few seconds ago," said Erasmus while attempting to catch his breath.

"What kind of snake was it," asked Daphne? "I'm not sure because I decided to hurry in and get Dad," said Erasmus breathing better.

"Was it red, black and yellow," asked Sammy on his way to the back door? "No it was more of a dusty, gray, brown color," answered Erasmus. "It could be a bull snake," said Daphne.

"Or it could be a rattler of one species or another," said Sammy.

"I hope our chickens, goats and Donkey Dan are safe," said momma skunk Daphne.

"I put the Beanie and the goats back in their pen as soon as I saw the snake," answered Erasmus as they entered the pasture gate.

"That was good thinking," remarked Sammy.

"I wish that I could have gotten the chickens into their pen but I didn't have any feed with me to entice them into the chicken yard," said Erasmus.

"What about Dan," asked Momma skunk.

"He never came out of his pen yet so I just shut the gate," answered Erasmus.

Now they were close to where the snake was so Sammy stopped with in eight foot of it. "It is most definitely a western diamond back," warned Sammy.

Sammy sent Erasmus to the barn to get his snake stick and a big burlap bag that was attached to a wire stand which held it open. The snaked coiled up and shook it's rattle which was missing a few buttons from it's tip. This was an older adult diamond back.

After two tries Sammy hooked the old guy and dropped him into the deep burlap. Then swiftly tying it tightly shut he took the bag and placed it in the back of his pickup truck bed. Sammy then drove far out into the forest where he released the old boy. Erasmus went along on the mission.

"Dad why did we release him instead of killing him," asked Erasmus.

"Sometimes it is best to catch them and release them where they can't harm anyone, if you have the tools for that available. Rattlesnakes mostly eat small mammals such as chipmunks, gophers, prairie dogs, rabbits, mice and rats. Many of these in the wild are disease carriers so the snakes help eliminate some of them. Besides this rattler was very old and doesn't have all that long to live. They live for about twenty years and I don't think he is far from that.

When they returned home the two guys noticed that the goats and Donkey Dan were back in the pasture. Upon entering the house Sammy walked into the dinning room and sat in the next to Daphne. Erasmus also plopped down at the table in a way which only a teenager could do. Meanwhile Bonkers who gave up on his vigil by the clock left the house by his newly installed kitty door. Levi the golden retriever raised his head mumbled what sounded like a humph and remained lying in the sun. Tremor noticing that the cat went out ran into the dinning room where he hid behind the china cabinet. It seemed like he always could tell when Sammy was about to tell what Tremor called a story.

"Perhaps you should've killed that snake," said momma skunk.

"Well I did have everything I needed to catch him and release him far from anyone, so that's what I decided to do," answered Sammy.

After all continued Sammy getting into a teaching mode, these snakes help eliminate rodents that may carry diseases. Tremor the wee house mouse was happy that it was taken far away from him because he didn't want to be the old snakes next meal.

"How many species of rattle snakes are there in Arizona," asked Daphne with a look of I'm sorry for the interruption on her face.

"I accept the look on your face smiled Sammy.

"You will just have to wait for the answer because I plan on telling you that a little farther along," said Sammy still smiling.

"What's the difference between the western diamond back, the adobe coon tail and the desert diamond back rattler," asked Erasmus.

"Not a thing at all because they are the same snake," answered Sammy.

"How big can they get," asked Daphne.

"They can reach seven feet long however it is rare to find one over six feet long. In fact most top out at five feet long," said Sammy.

Sammy asked Erasmus and momma skunk to allow him to continue his lecture without anymore interruptions. They both agreed to hold down the questions as best as they could. So he began again. The tail of the snake has from two to six black bands divided by a pale gray space which is why some call it the 'coon tail', even though the Mojave rattler and others also have those black bands. We have thirteen rattle snakes as far as we know in Arizona and here are the thirteen:

1. The western diamond back is the one we caught this morning and it is the biggest one in the western united states. It is also the one responsible for more deaths and bites than any of its fellow rattlers. They are found nearly all over Arizona.

2. The one called the western rattle snake is found in the northwestern part of Arizona. It gets about five feet long. It's venom is twice as strong than that of the diamond backs but it produces less of it.

3. Then we have the ridge nosed rattler he normally only gets close to two and one half feet in length. And by the way they are the official Arizona state reptile. It is one of the four species with special protection of the state of Arizona. You can locate this snake near the southern border of Arizona.

4. The next rattle snake is the twin spot and is another protected species. They grow to about two feet in length. The sound of it's rattle is so faint that it sounds like a cricket or other insect. It got it's name from the fact that it has twin spots running down its back from head to tail.

5. The Rock rattler is just under three foot long and it's tail changes color when it becomes an adult. The state has also put a special protection on them. You could find them in the south eastern part of our state.

6. Then the speckled rattle snake gets to about four and a half feet long. It's color varies according to it's surroundings. They are found on the western side of Arizona.

7. The Mohave rattler tops out at four and one half feet long. It lives in the Mohave desert From the western border to central Arizona and most of the southern portion of our state.

8. The Prairie rattle snake grows to nearly six foot. It covers the North eastern area of our Arizona state. It is said to be the snake used in the Hopi snake dance ceremony.

9. Then we have the black tail rattle snake that gets up to four feet long. It varies in color from beige, brown, green and golden.

10. The black rattler is under four feet long and its young are vividly patterned so they look different that the adults.

11. The tiger rattler reaches three foot long. It's venom is very powerful but it holds very little venom to inject.

12. This rattler and the diamond back are the two most well know rattle snakes. The sidewinder name came from the fact that it travels in a side winding motion. They barely reach over two feet long. He is the only rattle snake with horns over its eyes. You can see them in almost all parts of Arizona.

13. Our last species found in Arizona is the Massasugo that tops put under two foot long.

This one is also protected in our state. They are the most primitive form of the rattlesnake They live in the lower eastern corner of southern Arizona.

"That is a lot of rattlesnakes. How many different species are there in the Americas," asked Erasmus.

"I don't know but there is one to many," squeaked Tremor.

"There are thirty six species known to live in the Americas and like I said Arizona has thirteen of them which is more than any other state," said Sammy.

Rattlesnakes have glands that create venom glands and because of that along with it's specialized fangs, it can deliver a large amount of venom in a single bite. In just a few seconds they can leave a fatal bite of venom injected into a rodent. I once read that the mortality rate in humans is from ten to twenty percent. Yet despite the reputation to the contrary they are not overly aggressive and they normally warn about an imminent strike by rattling. The main enemies of the rattlesnake are retail hawks, eagles, coyotes, wild turkeys, roadrunners, and king snakes. "And me," mumbled Tremor the wee mouse quietly.

"Dad what should we do when we go hiking around this state," asked Erasmus?

"Here are a few things you should do," said Sammy.

1. Carry a phone. 2. Hike with at least one friend. 3. Always keep an eye open for snakes.

4. If you see a rattler back away slowly and quietly. 5. Carry a long walking stick out in front of you.

"I think its best not to go hiking in the wilderness so that you won't run into rattlesnake," said Daphne.

"I hate to have to tell you this but if you live near the edge of the desert, forest, mountain or even in a real populated area you could still run into a rattlesnake.

Realizing Sammy was finished Erasmus left for eddy beavers house and Daphne continued her house cleaning. Tremor went to the kitchen and left the house to look for seeds in the yard. In the meantime Sammy continued writing of his segment for the Donkey Dan Show. Which by the way was about the western diamond back.

So all was quiet in the old oak tree house.

THE HUNDRED LEGGED PROBLEM

EWALD AND HIS BUDDY RANDY were outside. Erasmus was playing chess in his room with Eddie beaver. Tremor was out in the yard collecting fruit from the orchard while still keeping and eye on Bonkers who was busy chasing butterflies in the pasture. Meanwhile Sammy was in the vegetable garden collecting some for lunch. Daphne was in the kitchen baking bread to have with their lunch. Suddenly the relative quiet was broken by her loud screams which caused Sammy to drop the vegetables and take off swiftly for the house. Erasmus and Eddie knocked over their chess board while getting up.

Ewald and Randy stopped playing catch and rushed toward the house. Tremor had no idea as to what happened so he hid behind the apple tree. Even old Bonkers the cat froze for a few minutes before continuing his butterfly chasing. Sammy ran into the kitchen just behind Erasmus and Eddie and noticing Daphne standing on a chair looked around trying to locate the reason for her screams.

"What is it and where is it," asked daddy skunk. It went under the stove.

"I don't know what it is but it has a hundred legs and it is ugly," answered momma skunk. "Are you sure it is under the stove," asked Erasmus as Ewald and Randy walked in. "What's going on," asked Ewald.

"Your mom saw some weird hundred legged creature go under the stove," said Eddie beaver.

"You're kidding," said Randy while looking nervously at the stove.

"Did that loud scream she let loose sound like she was kidding," asked Erasmus. "Okay guys lets stop the talking and solve the problem," suggested Sammy.

"About how long was this creature," asked Ewald.

"I'm not really sure but I think it was five feet long and very ugly," answered Daphne.

Naturally Sammy already had an idea as to what the hundred foot problem really is and it isn't five feet long.

"Erasmus you and Eddie be ready to move the stove out from the wall when I get back," said Sammy. "Why are you leaving," asked momma skunk. Sammy just left without answering her. In about three minutes he returned carrying a gallon jar and a two foot long stick.

"Everyone Else except Erasmus and Eddie leave the kitchen," said Sammy. When the three of them were the only ones left in the room he said, "Now boys move the stove." the stove moved away from the wall and on the floor was the problem of one hundred legs but with about eighty legs short of the hundred.

Of course it wasn't five feet long either. Sammy held the jar in front of it and used the stick to push it in the jars opening. Then he stood the jar up and placed the lid on it.

"It's a centipede," said Erasmus smiling.

"Yep it sure is," remarked Eddie.

"I hate centipedes," said Tremor looking on from the side of the refrigerator.

Sammy carried the jar into the living room where everyone else was sitting down waiting for the results of the hunt. Sammy, Erasmus and Eddie also took a seat as Sammy began to speak.

"Our one hundred legged unwelcome visitor is actually a centipede. Though the name centipede means one hundred feet, the Arizona giant has a lot less than one hundred, said Sammy. Then continuing he said, "this guy is about five inches long but they can get from 8 - 9 inches long. As you can see the one we trapped has a black head and tail, with a sort of orange colored body and yellow tan legs."

They have one pair of legs for each body segment. These characters have a pair of fang like, modified front legs which are full of venom. Their bites are very painful but for the most part not life threatening to people or large animals. The bold colors of orange and black of the giant Arizona centipede are a form of warning meant to scare away possible predators. However they also have another defense.

It's a tail end that appears like the head in color and it also has what looks like orange antennae but these are actually legs made to appear like antennae. The big guy can move swiftly either forward or backwards. If a predator mistakes its tail end for the front the can rapidly bend around to attack it using his venomous front legs.

"I have never seen one in the daytime," said Eddie.

"They are nocturnal, and hide in dark damp areas during the daylight hours. On humid nights they especially come out to hunt for their prey," answered Sammy.

Then continuing on with his lecture, in Arizona we mostly see them in the summer during what we call the monsoon season. The different species live in a variety of habitats the desert, the tropics and even the sea shore. They are found under rocks, logs, bark, under litter, and even in the soil. Our two desert species are found throughout the southern united states and Mexico.

"Do they have any enemies that hunt them," asked Ewald.

"As a matter of fact they do have a few, the ringtail cat, owls, coyotes, bobcats and badgers are the main ones," said daddy skunk.

"How long do they live," asked Randy.

It is estimated that they live only about five years," answered Sammy.

In our dry state you can often see them in landscaping with a high moisture content. Like the one we caught they can sometimes be found inside, normally in the kitchen, bathroom, basement or the crawl space under the house.

"What are you going to do with it," asked Ewald.

"I plan to drop him off far into the desert where he won't have much of a chance to scare anyone again," said Sammy.

"Good, I hate those ugly beast," squeaked Tremor loudly remembering that Bonkers was out chasing butterflies.

Daphne went back to cooking when Sammy and the boys left with the centipede.

And all was quiet in the old oak tree house.

DON'T INVITE THEM TO YOUR PICNIC

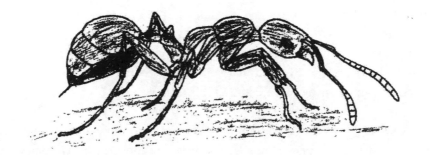

IT WAS FUN WHEN THE whole family went to visit relatives in Phoenix, that is for Bonkers and especially for Tremor mouse. When the family was gone Bonkers would take his cat nap in Sammy's chair because he couldn't get caught and scolded. Tremor liked it when they went to Phoenix because he could get out his skate board and dash all over the house. When the family first moved into the oak tree house Tremor was skate boarding through the living room and went right over bonkers tail, up his back and jumped off his nose. This caused the cat to screech out a cry scaring Sammy who fell out of bed onto the wood floor. When Sammy came out to see what was going on he just saw Bonkers dangling from the window drapes. Tremor couldn't believe he did that but he wasn't watching where he was going. But on days like this he had fun teasing the cat by skating right by him. Bonkers never was able to catch the little mouse.

While visiting their grandparents the boys decided to explore some of the fields and vacant lots. Erasmus went close to a field of alfalfa and noticed a large almost circular bare spot in the field. Being curious Ewald suggested they walk out into the field to check it out. Erasmus agreed so the two boys walked up to the bare circle and discovered a large ant colony. Later that afternoon they talked Sammy into going with them to look it over.

"Dad what are these big red ants," asked Erasmus.

"Are they those red invasive fire ants from south America," asked Ewald.

"Actually these ants are our Arizona native fire ants, Not the imported fire ants from south America," answered Sammy as ne continued with his lesson.

The south American fire ants sting as many as fourteen million people or more in the U.S. every year. They are a very aggressive species but so far they haven't appeared in Arizona yet as far as I know, perhaps it is because our climate is too dry for their taste.

The Arizona red fire ant is one of three fire ant species that inhabit the desert southwest. All three of these fire ant species are similar in color, size and shape. There are two sizes of workers in this colony with the larger one measuring about 1/3 rd of an inch. The queens are just a bit bigger than these large workers.

"You said queens plural instead of queen. Is there more than one in a colony," asked Erasmus.

"Yes they sometimes have more than one queen in a colony," said Sammy. You will notice that the ants have a sort of orange- red head and mid section with a black or darker abdomen. May times they are just completely red- orange all over which is the case at this ant mound.

"Are they just found in Arizona," asked Ewald.

"Not at all, they cover the widest area of all three of the native species, Answered Daddy Skunk continuing the lecture.

They occur across all of the southern united states from Carolina, through parts of Tennessee, Kansas and all the way to California. You can see them in New Mexico, Texas and of course here.

"How can they be killed," asked Erasmus.

"When I lived in the Phoenix area two friends and I grew Alfalfa. in one area of our field was a big nest so we purchased some powdered cyanide. We dug down a foot or so and buried the powder, covered it over and irrigated the field. The water caused the powder to turn into gas which killed the ants. I guess we got their queens also because that was the last we ever saw of them.

"These days you can't purchase it," said Sammy.

"I can see why it isn't available anymore," said Erasmus.

"So can I actually," added Sammy before continuing.

Regardless of the method you use the object is to kill the queen or queens. They are the only ant in the colony able to lay eggs and keep the colony numbers up. So dead queen dead colony though it may take several weeks after she dies that the colony dies out.

Another place I've seen them is around barrel cacti collecting bits of the fruit especially those that have dropped off already.

"Do they have any predators," asked Erasmus.

"They sure do," was Sammy's quick answer. Many birds, insect eating mammals, some snakes, spiders, centipedes and lizards find them tasty treats," said daddy skunk continuing as they walked back to the house of Daphne's parents.

"When I was in fifth or sixth grade I had some pet horned lizards. I often captured some ants of this species to feed them," said Sammy.

"Didn't they get stung," asked Ewald.

"If they did the horned toads thick hide must have protected them from the ant stings," answered Sammy as they entered the house.

And all was quiet at the grand parents house but not at the old oak tree house where bonkers was chasing Tremor as he skate boarded from room to room. Bonkers slid around corners crashing into the walls but he never got close to catching the wee mouse.

After Tremor ducked behind the grandfather clock it became quiet again.

THE CORAL AND THE KING

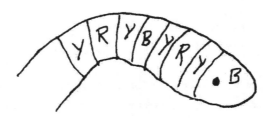

CORAL

B= Black

Y= Yellow

R= Red

Arizona King

W= White or Cream

R=Red

B=Black

Y= Yellow or Cream

"**D**AD COME OVER HERE AND look at this bright colored snake," said Erasmus.

Sammy and little Ewald walked over to see what Erasmus was talking about. Sammy knew what it was right away and he killed it with his shovel.

"Why did you kill it," asked Ewald.

"We have many dangerous and venomous things in Arizona and this is one of the worst of the bunch," said Daddy Skunk.

"It's not a rattle snake so what is it," asked Erasmus.

"This snake is the Sonoran Coral Snake and it is one of the three species found it the U.S. this guy was around nineteen inches long but they can get up to twenty four inches in length," said Sammy.

The Sonoran inhabits nearly half of our state and they are related to the cobra family of snakes. There are a few myths about these snakes out there. Here are two of those:

1. Since the coral snakes have very small mouths they can only bite your loose skin between your fingers. This is not true at all. It will and can bite any part of your body that it can reach.

2. Coral snakes have their fangs in the rear of their mouths and have small teeth. This means they have to chew on you to inject their venom. The idea being that if you get it before it starts to chew it can't inject the venom.

"This is also not true, it's fangs are in the front of the mouth. Though they do tend to chew it's not needed to inject the venom which is injected with the first bite," said Sammy.

"How can you tell it's a coral snake," asked Ewald.

"Well even though there are a few exceptions still the best way is by their color pattern," answered Sammy.

Their face is solid black, followed by yellow, red, and yellow bands which go all around it's body. Just remember this old saying; red and yellow kills a fellow. If you see that combination of black, red, yellow, and yellow leave it alone. These snakes have very small eyes which are hard to see on a very black face.

"Have you run across very many of these coral snakes," asked Ewald.

"Not counting this one only a couple in my entire life," Answered Sammy.

"Exactly how dangerous is this species of coral snake," asked Erasmus.

"They may be known for a mild temperament but their venom is very dangerous," said daddy skunk.

I suggest that you not become careless with them but instead treat them as you would any other venomous snake, very carefully. Being bitten by one can be very scary and deadly.

"More so than the diamond back rattle snake," asked Ewald.

"Yes because the coral snake anti -venom has gone way past its expiration date. This is because of the fact that so many few people are bitten that the serum was deemed too expensive to produce.

"So at this time there isn't any anti -venom," said Sammy.

"So what can we do if we see one like this coral snake," asked Ewald.

"Just simply leave it alone or if I'm nearby come and get me," instructed Sammy.

The boys both left to tell their friends what they learned. Sammy finished what he was doing and went into the old oak tree house.

And all was quiet in the old oak tree house.

THE KING

A WEEK AFTER THE RUN IN with the Arizona coral snake Sammy placed his goats on ropes attached to their collars outside the pasture fence. He did this once before so that they would eat the weeds, shrubs and grass from against the fence. However that time it turned out badly. A big English sheep dog running loose came down the path through the lot and tried to herd the goats like it would a flock of sheep. Sheep dogs can't herd goats because the goats will normally just run off in as many directions as there are animals. The sheep dog bounded up the path and scared the goats who couldn't get away so Sammy had to go out and chase it off and bring his goats back into the pasture. Today he had a plan, he placed his one goat who wasn't scared of the dog out half way down the path. He knew that when Beanie was a very young kid goat that she was raised with two just weaned German Sheppard puppies. So the pups thought of her as just an odd looking sister.

"Dad why is Beanie so far from the other goats," asked Ewald.

Sammy explained his whole plan to Ewald and ended by saying, "She learned to play ruff like a puppy from day one. The two dogs treated her like another dog for two years and she learned how to defend herself against them by playing ruff right back.

"Is that why her horns are cut half way off and flat instead of pointed," asked the little roadrunner?.

"Yes that's why," answered Sammy.

"That prevented her from accidentally goring the dogs right dad," asked Erasmus.

"That sheep dog running at our goats could cause them to get hurt very badly," said Daphne walking up.

Everyone watched from the back porch as that big English sheep dog came bounding up the path right at old beanie not realizing that she wasn't scared and wouldn't move. She no doubt thought he wanted to play with her. Just as he got close enough to her she lowered her head up under his mid section.

She did this so fast he never knew what hit him. Then she raised him up swiftly and tossed him over her back. As soon as he landed on the ground he tucked his tail and ran off. Tremor who was watching the whole thing from under donkey Dan fell over with laughter. In fact the whole family laughed even donkey Dan who let out a loud heehawseveral times.

"I don't think he will be back for a long time if ever," said momma skunk.

As they all headed back to the house Ewald looked to his left and yelled, "snake". Sammy picked up his shovel from the gate and walked toward the snake. When he was about thirty inches away he saw the tricolor pattern of red, black, yellow, black of the king snake.

"It's okay this one is a Mountain king snake and though he can bite he hasn't any fangs or venom. "I don't care what he is I do not like snakes," said momma skunk as she quickened her steps toward the house.

"Me either," remarked Tremor the mouse as he dashed toward his entrance to the house. "I thought the king snake was black and white banded," said Erasmus.

"Actually there are seven or perhaps eight species of king snakes from Canada throughmost of the United States," said Sammy. The black and white banded one is the one most often seen in our area and it is called the California king snake. This species inhabits central to southeastern Arizona.

"I have seen a few in the Phoenix area when I was young," said daddy skunk.

"Do they make good pets," asked Ewald? "Yes but it's best to leave them in the wild," said Sammy.

"Why is that," asked Ewald.

"Because they eliminate a lot of small rodents for one thing and I'll tell you more about that later," answered Sammy.

"Have you ever heard the saying, red face, your safe," asked Sammy.

"No," said Ewald and Erasmus together.

"Well if the snake has a red face it isn't the venomous coral snake so it is safe.

"However if red is touching yellow you're a dead fellow," said daddy skunk.

The king snake has the largest range of any North American snake. Being extremely adaptable for a reptile they make themselves a home in a wide range of habitats. Most of their kind are very secretive and hide in places like dense vegetation or inside the dens of rodents. They prefer to stay on the ground but they can climb into bushes or swim in a pond or slow moving stream.

"What do they eat," asked Ewald.

"Now that you brought it up here is the main reason to allow them to stay a non-captive," said Daddy skunk.

They mostly hunt during the morning hours close to sunrise or the hours just before sunset. His menu consist of frogs, small birds, small rodents, lizards, the eggs of birds or reptiles.

"However here is the reason to leave them in the wild. They feed on other snakes such as the rattlesnake, copperhead, cotton mouth, and coral snake," said Sammy.

"You mean that they can eat those venomous snakes," asked Erasmus.

"That practice is what makes the king snake so exceptional among snakes and earned then the family name of king snake," said Sammy smiling.

"But why aren't they killed by the venomous snakes," asked Ewald.

"Yes, why aren't they bitten and die from it," added Erasmus.

"The king snakes are immune to the venom of these snakes," said daddy skunk.

Rattlesnakes can identify the king snakes by smell and will normally retreat as fast as they can. The Arizona mountain king is a medium sized snake of about 3 ½ to for feet long. They have as you can see on our friend there have alternating red, black, and white or cream bands. The cream bands are bordered by black so red is not touching 'yellow'.

The Arizona mountain king snake do well in three thousand to nine thousand feet. They often try a bluff on animals and humans as a defense. What they do is coil up and vibrate their tail. Some of the creatures they prey on them are hawks, roadrunners, raccoons, and badgers.

"I see our king snake got bored and slithered off," said Sammy.

The guys headed into the house. And all was quiet in the old tree house.

THE EIGHT LEGGED WHAT?

I t was Halloween and Sammy had just driven into the driveway when Daphne let out a blood curdling scream. Erasmus was at Eddie beavers house but Ewald ran out to the kitchen to find out what was wrong. Daphne was gone so he ran into the living room but she was nowhere to be found. So he dashed out into the back yard just in time to see momma skunk telling Sammy that there was a small tarantula in the kitchen under the table. Ewald only heard that something was under the table.

As Sammy went into the house he thought to himself, "We sure have a lot of excitement around here". It took him only a second to locate the spider which he trapped with a glass jar. Then he took it out the front door and carried it to the forest where he let it loose. Ewald ran after Sammy but still never saw what made momma skunk scream so loud. By the time he caught up the spider was making it's way deep into a thicket.

"What was it," asked Ewald.

"It was only an eight legged wolf," answered Sammy.

"Only an eight legged. What," said Ewald.

Sammy laughing said, "It was only a wolf spider a very agile hunter with great eye sight. Lets go in and I'll tell you about the eight leggede wolf," said Daddy skunk.

After they all were seated Sammy started to tell the wolf Spider facts or at least what he knew. These guys are lone hunters that live alone and they don't spin webs. Sometimes they pounce on prey as they find it or they may even chase it over a short distance like wolves do. Or they might lay in wait for prey and ambush it.

"Are they dangerous to us," asked Ewald.

"Well when the female has an egg case attached to her spinnerets you should stay away from her because she will bite. I can tell you it does hurt but that pain goes away pretty quickly. Their venom does not harm us because it is made for their small prey," said Sammy.

The wolf spider has eight eyes arranged in three rows, six are small and you may not see them unless your close to the spider but two are large and visible. These eyes give the wolf spider very good vision. They also have an acute sense of touch thanks to the hair on their legs and body. Since they depend on camouflage for protection their coloring is matched to the surrounding habitat. Ewald left to go to Randy's house and Sammy went to bag up candy for all the trick or treaters that might come at dusk.

"I don't think I would like being bitten by that wolf spider so I hope Sammy took it far away," said Tremor.

And all was quiet in the old oak tree house.

NOT WILEY- E- COYOTE

Bonkers the cat was asleep on the window sill and Tremor was behind the grandfather clock eating his lunch. Daphne was gone visiting her friend grandma squirel. Erasmus was at Eddie beavers house playing a video game. Sammy was outside feeding the chickens, goats and donkey Dan. Levi the dog was asleep under the mulberry tree.

Ewald and Randy were on the floor watching a roadrunner cartoon. It was the one where Wile-E-Coyote puts a fake railroad track section across the road. Then he hides the ends with bushes and puts on a disguise after which he holds up a sign that reads railroad crossing stop. The roadrunner runs right past him knocking him down. As he is lying on the fake track he ears a train coming and looks up just in time to see it hit him. Then you see the bird on the back of the train and below him is the words 'The End'.

The next cartoon was interrupted by Levi barking, donkey Dan Heehawing, and Sammy yelling get out of hear and even louder beat it. By the time the boys got outside whatever it was that caused the commotion was gone.

"You better run," yelled Sammy as the guys walked up.

"What happened and who better run," asked Ewald.

"A coyote tried to get into the hen house as I was about to feed the goats. Donkey Dan let me know about it right away and helped to scare it off," answered daddy skunk.

"We were just watching the roadrunner taking care opf old Wile-E- Coyote," said Randy. "I really have always liked that cartoon," said Sammy. Dad are coyotes dangerous to people, "asked Ewald.

"Suppose we go on the porch and I'll tell you everything I know about coyotes," said Sammy.

The three guys walked up onto the porch and sat down in the porch chairs. Meanwhile Tremor came outside and hid behind his boulder by the porch because he realized Sammy was about to begin a nature story.

Coyotes are canines and are native to north American. They are close relatives to the gray wolf. But unlike that silly Wile-E-Coyote the real coyote is smart, versatile, able to adapt to and expand into human modified environments. They can be found in large urban areas in cities like Chicago. In Arizona you can find them in Phoenix and the surrounding cities. They are known for jumping over fences even six foot high in Sun City where they attack small dogs like poodles or Chihuahuas. I have seen a coyote run up behind two women walking their small dog and grabbing the dog leash and all.

Coyotes seldom attack an adult human unless that person is dying or the coyote is rabid. The coyote is a very intelligent canine. They have been seen watching a badger digging at a rodents den and they kept watch at the other entrance waiting for the rodent to exit. In that way they steal the badgers meal without a fight. It is flexible in it's social organization living in a family unit or in loosely knit packs. Their diet is varied of mostly animal meat, including rabbits, hares, birds, rodents, deer, reptiles, and fish, though they also eat fruit, and vegetables. In the winter when meat is scarce in the Arizona coyotes will eat mesquite beans which are high in protein. Humans are the worst threat to the coyotes followed by gray wolves and cougars. Coyotes have been known to mate with the eastern gray wolves and the hybrid offspring are known by the name of 'coy wolf'.

The coyote is often mentioned in native American folklore, mostly as a trickster. During the European colonization, it was treated as a cowardly and untrustworthy animal. Today their image hasn't changed attitudes toward the coyote remain negative for the most part. "How big do they get," asked Ewald?

"The males get up to 45 pounds while the females top out at about 40 pounds," answered Sammy.

The color of their fur varies but it is normally a light gray and red mixed with black and white. They have a soft under coat with course, long guard hairs. In general they have a white face mask and a bushy tail. The coyote is shorter than the gray wolf but it does have longer ears. When they are waking or running they tend to hold their tail in a downwards position unlike the wolf who carries his straight outwards.

"Are their tracks like those of a dog," asked Randy.

"No they are less rounded in shape," said Sammy.

"He will be back right dad," said Ewald.

"I'm sure he will," stated Sammy.

"How are you going to keep him out of the chicken house," asked Randy.

"I have a secret weapon," said Sammy smiling.

"Is it a gun, a trap or what," asked Ewald.

'It is a white guard that I will put in the chickens pen every night until that coyote comes back," said daddy skunk.

"What do you mean until he comes back," asked Ewald.

"Do you recall what Beanie did to the sheep dog that time," asked Sammy.

"Oh, I see when he returns he will get the surprise of his life and will never come back again," said Ewald.

"That's the idea," said Daddy skunk.

The boys went back to the television set to watch more roadrunner cartoons. Tremor went back into the house also but not before saying, "I don't like coyotes but I pity that one if he comes back".

Sammy took Beanie from the goast pen and placed her in the chicken pen along with some hay.

And all was quiet in the old oak tree house.

A HOUSE CAT IT'S NOT

S AMMY WAS AT THE RADIO station doing his broadcast on the Donkey Dan Show. His science fact was on the Arizona bobcat. Daphne, Erasmus, Ewald, Randy raccoon and Eddie beaver were all in the living room of the old oak tree house listening to the show. Tremor who was barely behind the clock was also listening to Sammy's story. Bonkers was outside playing with a cricket and could care less about the radio show, he was only thinking of what he was doing. Sammy always opened with the line, "This is Sammy the daddy skunk of the farmer family album". Then after the opening he would announce what his story was about. Today's story is called, 'Its not a house cat'.

Even though it is on the decline in numbers because of humans moving into the natural habitats of the bobcat, our Arizona bobcat is still our most common wild feline. The biggest Arizona feline is naturally the mountain lion but the bobcats outnumber them in Arizona. Bobcats are a medium size cat weighing in at about thirty pounds. The average adults length is two and one half feet long. Even though they are wild and sort of dangerous they still are very beautiful creatures that are varied in color from gray to orange with black markings and undersides that are white. The bobcat has pointed ears with tufts on the ends. His tail is a short five inches which is where the name bobcat comes from. Normally bobcats are timid and try to avoid human contact. However don't allow yourself to be fooled by their small size. They are very strong and do bring down small deer. Also they are ferocious when they feel challenged, so never walk toward one to get a better look. They may appear like a cute large friendly house cat but they can cause serious damage with their claws and sharp teeth.

"Dad is really on a roll on today's show," remarked Ewald.

They can be found all throughout Arizona at all elevations from desert to rocky and forested areas. Human neighborhoods are constantly expanding into the natural habitats of these and other animals. So don't be surprised if you see a bobcat lying in you backyard or in your rose garden. Unfortunately hunting and trapping the Arizona bobcat is legal in this state and is another factor in their decline in numbers.

Remember bobcats are carnivores like your tabby cat and prefer a meat diet. Their food of choice is rabbits, which multiply as they say like rabbits.

"If they are cats mice are on their menu also," squeaked Tremor. Predators of the bobcat are plentiful and include the mountain lion, foxes, coyotes wolves, birds of prey like the owl and naturally humans.

Their life expectancy is twelve to fifteen years in the wild. Well that is our show for today but be sure to tune in next Sunday morning to hear momma skunk Daphne.

"That was a good show and dad picked out three good songs to play before his bobcat facts segment," said Erasmus.
"Yes it was very well done," remarked Eddie.
"I thought it was purr- fect but it makes me want to go out and start a save our bobcat from extinction lobbying group at the Arizona capital," said Daphne skunk.
"I liked it also but I also like your play on the word perfect mom," said Ewald.

And then all was quiet in the old oak tree house at least until Sammy came home.

COMING BACK GRADUALLY

"DAD I READ THAT ARIZONA has a gray wolf population and they are planning on adding more," stated Erasmus. "I understand that the state of Arizona is thinking about placing captive born wolf pups with wild packs instead of releasing pairs to form new packs.

The Mexican gray wolf was on the edge of extinction and is still in deep water. Sometime in the 1970's the breeding program started with the last seven wolves that survived. Now they are protected under the endangered species act w3hich allows people to scare them away in a non- injurious fashion. They can be scared away by making loud noises with any thing handy.

"Can you throw rocks at them," asked Ewald.
"I don't believe you can but you might be able to throw rocks in their general direction.
"Has anyone been attacked by one of the Mexican wolves in Arizona," asked Erasmus.

Hunters have reported that seeing and hearing wolves hasn't affected their success at hunting game. there is of last count fifty wolves roaming the ten thousand square miles of the wolf recovery area of the Fort Apache Reservation. It is not a good idea to feed curious wolves that come near your camp but they normally try to avoid human contact.

"What should you do if one comes toward you," asked Ewald.
"Well the best thing is, do not ever run and always face them. Then raise your arms and try to make yourself look as big as possible. Throwing rocks and yelling loudly does work to scare them away," instructed Sammy. Their was a new proposal to release Mexican gray wolves in Yavapai county.
"I knew someone who had a half Mexican wolf mixed different subspecies of gray wolf. That pup was very timid and would hide if a stranger walked into the house.
"I have a hard time picturing a timid wolf," said Daphne.
"How can you tell a coyote from the Mexican wolf," asked Erasmus.
"The ears are different, the coyotes are longer and pointed. The wolf has rounded shorter ears. Also the coyote has a more pointed nose while the wolf has a large blocky nose. Wolves also have a stiffer and different gate than the coyote which walks with a more of a bounce and bounding gate. Coyotes are skittish where a wolf displays a curious behavior," said daddy skunk.

The grandfather clock struck nine o'clock and everyone went off to bed. Except Bonkers the cat who slept in the fall sunshine all day.

And all was quiet in the old oak tree house.

LIONS, BEARS, BUT NO TIGERS

SAMMY WAS SITTING IN HIS chair eating an apple for a snack. Bonkers was outside in the pasture chasing what looked like a pocket gopher. Erasmus was on the couch reading his biology chapter for school. Ewald was at Randy raccoon's house because Randy and his parents just returned from a visit to his grand parents in the mountains in south eastern Arizona. Ewald couldn't wait for his pal Randy to come over so he went to Randys.

Daphne left after breakfast to visit her friend grandma Squirrel for the day. Tremor was out collecting some dry corn from the chicken pen to place in his winter storage. He knew he was one lucky mouse living in such a food rich house.

"What did you do at your grandparents house," asked Ewald.

"Mostly dad and I explored the borderland between Arizona and Mexico," said Randy. "Did you see any of the animals my dad has told us about or featured on his radio program," asked Ewald.

"Well we saw several rattlesnakes, a bobcat, a javelina, a big hairy old taratula, centipedes and scorpions," Randy told his pal Ewald. Then he said, "We saw a very strange big cat, my dad said it looked kind of like a spotted mountain lion,".

"Wow, I'll bet my dad will know what it is," said Ewald.

"That is what I planned on doing, so lets get going," ordered Randy.

The two friends headed out right away to go ask Sammy about this odd mountain lion. In the meantime Tremor was in the process of taking his dried corn behing the old grandfathrer clock. Erasmus was reading the last two pages of his assigned biology chapter and Bonkers finally giving up on catching that pocket gopher came into the living room to take a much needed cat nap on the window sill. When the guys entered they both started talking at the same time.

"Whoa, I can't understand you because your both talking at the same time," stated Sammy. Then continuing he said, "Is this something that happened on Randys visit"? "Yes," They both said at the same time.

"Okay, Ewald suppose we let Randy tell it," said Sammy smiling.

"Well began the little raccoon my dad and I had just rounded a big boulder at the edge of a small canyon when we looked up and noticed a big cat lying on the top of a group of huge boulders".

"Was it a mountain lion," asked Sammy.

"Dad said it didn't look like any mountain lion he ever saw before," answered Randy.

"I know that your dad has seen plenty of mountain lions before," remarked Sammy getting even more curious.

"He said that this one was spotted and had a broad head," said Randy.

"That sounds oddly familiar," said daddy Skunk.

"What do you think it was," asked Ewald?.

"Well if I'm right I believe it is a top level carnivore with powerful jaws that hasn't been seen in the U.S. for many years. In fact it is thought to be extinct in North America," said Sammy.

"Where else can they be found and what are they called," asked an excited Ewald.

"Do you guys recall what Dorthy kept saying before she met the cowardly lion on the yellow brick road," asked Sammy.

"No," said both boys at once.

"She kept saying, "Lions, tigers and bears," said Sammy. "Then continuing he began a short lecture. If she would have been in Arizona on our highway interstate ten Instead of OZ, she would have said, "Lions, bears but no tigers," smiled Sammy at an attempt to be funny.

"You can't think it was a tiger," said Randy.

"Let me answer it this way, she would have said Lions, Jaguars and bears," said Sammy all proud of himself.

"But if they are considered extinct in north America where else are they," asked Ewald for the second time.

To get here they would've had to travel from south America through Mexico, so to answer that question south America. It is the largest cat in the Americas and once roamed from Argentina all the way to the Grand Canyon. Today they are endangered all through their rage but thought to be extinct in the U.S.

Like I said, "They are a top level carnivore that helps overgrazing of plants by herbivores,". They are known to eat javelina, deer, snakes, monkeys, sloths, crocodiles, tapirs, frogs, fish and just about anything else they can catch. Their color varies somewhat. But normally they are tan or a yellow with spots and rosette shapes over nearly their entire body. It is at home in a very wide variety of habitats including mountain scrub land, swamps, rainforest, and the pampas grasslands of Argentina as well as other habitats. Jaguars live and hunt alone and a males range can be from 20 - 60 square miles.

The male does aggressively protect his home turf and it's resident females from other males. They mostly hunt on the ground but they sometimes climb trees to pounce on prey. They have very powerful jaws that can deliver a crushing bite to an animals skull killing it. They also unlike other felines their size love to swim in water hunting for fish.

"Are their foot prints the same as a mountain lions," asked Randy.

"They are similar to a mountain lions but the heel pad is too big and the toes too close to the back pad," said Sammy.

"Randy would it be okay for me to use your adventure on this Sundays radio broadcast of the Donkey Dan Show," asked Sammy.

"Yes my dad would love that and we will be listening for sure," said Randy as he and Ewald left to tell his parents about this Sundays show. Tremor heard the whole thing and said, "Another animal that would eat me if it could,". Erasmus Said, "I think it would be a good broadcast because people are interested in saving the endangered creatures in our state and elsewhere". Sammy walked over to the table with paper and pencil in hand.

And all was quiet in the old oak tree house once more.

STEALTH ON FOUR PAWS

*S*AMMY WAS GIVING A LECTURE at Ewalds school on one of Arizona's dangerous Animals. For this nature science lecture he chose the mountain lion or as some call it the puma. As usual Ewald was a little excited having his dad at his school and though he wouldn't admit it to anyone he really like it. The students were polite and listened to what he was telling them. The boys were especially listening intently at what was being said.

Years ago Sammy learned that people remember more and listen better when you use visual things that they can see and not just words. He firmly believes in the saying that a picture is worth a thousand words and today reinforced that in his mind. He began by saying, "Today I will tell you some facts about the biggest cat in Arizona who also is the second heaviest cat in the Americas behind the south American Jaguar."

Then he went on, The mountain lion also called the cougar, puma and panther is found in north America from Canada to Mexico and from there through central and into south America. They are well known for their strength and stealth.

"Does anyone here know if mountain lions roar like the African lions do," asked Sammy. One young fellow raised his hand so Sammy called on him.

"My father told me that the couldn't roar," said the boy.

"That's right the mountain lion like the house cat cannot roar instead they hiss, growl, spit and if your lucky purr," stated Sammy.

A little girl raised her hand so Sammy called on her next. "I don't think I would like to take the chance on finding out if I could make a mountain lion would purr for me," she said.

"Me either," said Sammy.

Here is a tape of what a mountain lion I asked about this had to say. Many of the students jumped when the cat on the tape let out a very loud roar. "Oops, wrong lion tape," said Sammy laughing. The students loved the joke that he pulled on them.

Mountain lions only eat meat and will eat anything it can catch and kill. In our state of Arizona it means they hunt elk, antelope, deer, desert bighorn sheep, wild horses, wild burros, and sometimes domestic animals like cattle, goats, sheep and horses. The cougar is an ambush hunter and can sneak up on it's prey on stealthy paws. They use a killing style that has them leaping on the preys back with a bite to the neck cutting off it's air. The mountain lion is a solitary animal except for a mother with kittens. These cats are strong, agile and sleek. If you happen to see a lone kitten back away slowly and leave the area. The adults color is tawny but may have red tones and light patches on it's under side. The little ones are born cute with blue eyes, spotted and with rings on their tails.

The adults with their large paws and powerful legs can jump 18 - 20 feet up and can go 40 feet across say a ravine. Since people are building in lion territories the cats overlap with people. Although attacks on humans are rare they do happen so if you run into one in the wild do not corner it or tease it. If you are or feel you are threatened try to make yourself look bigger and scary, also steadily keep eye contact, shout loudly but calmly while flaring out your jacket which will make you look larger. Slowly back away while staring into it's eyes. Never ever run or play dead or you might be. If attacked protect your neck and use rocks or thick sticks to fight back. A good long knife is the best weapon for close contact.

"I once was in a tiny valley called hidden valley in the south mountain area south of Phoenix when I was sixteen it was winter and I was alone.

I recall to this day the feeling that something was watching me. I was sure it wasn't a coyote since I heard no coyote calls or answers. It was so quiet because the birds stopped chirping and flying around the water holes," said Sammy realizing he had all of their attention. Ewald getting into it asked, "Could it have been a jaguar like Randy and his dad saw on their visit to his grandparents?" "Could be after all anything is possible but at the time I thought it might be a mountain lion," said Sammy.

Another girl raised her hand and changed the subject by asking, "How old can they live to". "Normally in the wild they can live up to 13 years old but a few have been found that were estimated to be 18 years old. The mountain lions only real predator is humans.

With that Sammy had finished his facts on the cougar and told the students to listen in on Sunday because his show was going to be about the 600 pound mah-TOH. The teacher thanked him for presenting his Arizona Mountain Lion Facts. When Sammy entered the old Oak tree house Daphne asked, "How did it go and did you use that tape?" "It went real well and I know the tape gave me all of their attention," said a happy daddy skunk.

Tremor hearing that squeaked, "Gosh I wish I could have gone with somehow".

Bonkers being a cat could've cared less.

And all was quiet in the old oak tree house until the boys got home from school.

MAH-TOH?

THE NEXT DAY AFTER SAMMY'S mountain lion lecture at Ewald's School was the Saturday before his mah-TOH broadcast on the Donkey Dan Show on the KLKY Radio station. Ewald was beside himself with curiosity as to what this mah-TOH might be. Finally after dinner he couldn't wait any longer and asked, "Dad what is a mah-TOH,"?

"The word is from the Lakota 'Sioux' dialect and means Bear," smiled daddy Skunk who knew Ewald would break down and ask sometime before going to bed.

"You'll have to wait until the broadcast to learn more, it's too close to bed time now, said Sammy.

After breakfast and Sammy left the entire family sat down near the radio to hear the show. This naturally included a wee mouse named Tremor who was hiding behind the grandfather clock nibbling on some popcorn. Tremor as always after the show ended will run out and tell donkey Dan and Beannie the goat about the show. Bonkers was outside chasing his tail in the pasture for lack of anything else to chase.

After three songs and a commercial Sammy started with, mah-TOH is the Sioux word in the 'Lakota' dialect for the bear. The Arizona Black bear is the most common bear in north America and is the smallest. In fact it is for the most part the only one still found in the lower forty eight states and for sure in Arizona. Males reach about 7 feet tall standing on their back legs. A large male can weigh up to 600 pounds or more. The females get up to about 400 pounds. They are solitary animals for the most part. Their main diet is berries, roots, insects cactus fruits and unfortunately livestock on occasion. And like the old cartoon bear Yogi they enjoy raiding camp sites for picnic baskets.

"Levi does that, if we are outside snacking on anything he will want a share," said Ewald. "Even if it's full of hot peppers," added Erasmus.

Black bears live about 30 years or so. They prefer elevations of 4,000 to 10,000 feet in forested areas that are lightly or heavily treed. They claim areas of about fifty square miles. Frequent sightings occur even around Prescott city proper. During drought they wander into towns looking for food. In fact they have been seen in the metro area of Phoenix which is below sea level. Other items on their menu are nuts, fish, small animals, some larger prey, dead animals and they will go through campers garbage. They may appear slow but when the need arises they cam run at a top speed of 35 to 40 miles an hour. They like to swim and climb trees. The bears claws are more dangerous in most cases than their bite. Black bears are very capable of opening screw top jars and opening door latches. They are extremely strong and can turn over heavy rocks. Their fur is soft with a very dense under coat and long guard hairs. They range in color from jet black to chocolate, cinnamon, blond and white and a few shades in between. They have a very good sense of smell in fact it is seven times stronger than that of a blood hound which is why old Yogi can locate those picnic baskets so easily. As far as attacks on humans the bear tries to avoid human contact as much as possible. The majority of black bear attacks take place in national parks where people just cannot seem to resist feeding them or trying to get a picture with a mother that has cubs. So if you see a Arizona black bear near your cabin or camp remember be safe, 'Do not feed Yogi bear'.

"What a great show," said Erasmus.
"Really good," said Daphne.
"I especially liked the ending where dad says to be safe and don't feed the Yogi bear," said Ewald.

And all was quiet in the old oak tree house.

Printed in the United States
By Bookmasters